Mystic Warriors:

Flame's Story

MYSTIC WARRIORS:

FLAME'S STORY

L.B. CARTER

Mystic Warriors: Flame's Story

Linda B. Carter
mtnlass1950@gmail.com

ISBNs:
979-8-9902090-0-8 (softcover)
979-8-9902090-1-5 (eBook)

Printed in the United States of America

Cover and Interior design: 1106 Design

I want to thank my son; without his support,
I wouldn't have been able to get this book published.
I want to thank my group of Sisters for putting up with me
throughout the process of writing, editing,
and holding my hand.

TABLE OF CONTENTS

Cast of Characters

Mystic Warriors
Denton, New Mexico

President

Thomas "Seer" O'Donnell

Telepathic, Precognition, Brother of Flame

Vice-President

Quinn "Torch" O'Shay

Telepathic, Fire Mage

Enforcer

William "Mountain" Wilcox

Telepathic, Earth Mage, Contractor

Secretary

Robert "Scribe" Sells

Photographic memory

Treasurer

Farris "Money" Anderson

CPA, Number wizard

Road Captain

Ogden "Spokes" Mayo

Navigator

IT Specialist

Jack "Wire" Harris

Computer wizard, Electrical mage

Medical Doctor

Drake "Doc" Stafford

Heals with conventional medicine and touch

Member

Michael "Viper" York

Telepathic, Corpsman, Snake whisperer

Prospect

David "Groundhog" Vail

Ultra-sensitive hearing, Ex-CIA black op

Prospect

James "Cyclone" Stone

Wind mage

Prospect

Andrew "Leach" Cannon

Ex-Para-rescue, Herbalist

xi

Cook

William "Tater Tot" Jones

Retired Army, Le Cordon Bleu Chef

Tater Tot's assistants

ELEMENTAL SPIRITS

President

Kelly "Roar" Bear

Speaks, reads, and writes all languages, human and animal.

Vice-President

Phoenix "Flame" O'Donnell

Telepathic, Fire mage, Fabricator

Secretary

Karen "Ink" Williams

Photographic memory, Expert forger

Treasurer

Susan "Stocks" Maynard

Numbers' mage

Business Manager

Brianna "Rain" Masters

Storm mage

Medical Doctor

Florence "Patch" Queen

Surgeon, Conventional medicine. Healing touch

IT Specialist

Liza "Ghost" Walker

> Computer expert, able to surf the Web undetected.

Advisor

Stacy "Oracle" Newman

> Psychic visions, Precognition

Member

Mary "Dex" Standford

> Earth mage, Contractor

Prospect

Anne "Terra" Turner

> Earth mage, Potter

Prospect

Abby "Aura" Johnson

> Aura reader, Combat medic, RN

PREQUEL

Phoenix looked up at the tall man standing in the open hospital-room door and recognized her brother. Even though he was taller and more heavily muscled, with broad shoulders and a beard, she saw the same caring hazel eyes from her childhood.

"Oh, Tommy. I'm so glad you came here," she cried as she was enfolded within his warm hug.

"I had already put in my retirement papers. Then I had a dream that Grandma was calling me home, and I immediately reached out to my Commanding Officer. My unit has several individuals with special gifts like mine, so he understood the sense of urgency. So, he fast-tracked my discharge papers for me, but they still had to go through channels."

"How is she doing, Sis?" Tommy asked, as he looked over at the woman beneath the covers.

"I think she was holding on until you could get here, Tommy. Go to her—she's awake but just resting her eyes," Phoenix told her brother softly.

He nodded and walked quietly up to the bed and laid his strong, tanned hand on the tiny blue-veined hand of his grandmother's.

"Hi, Grandma. I made it here for you," he said.

Opening her faded blue eyes, the frail old woman smiled. "I knew you would be here. I knew you would hear me calling. I wanted to see and talk with you one last time before I join your grandfather.

"I told him he had to wait just a little longer because I knew you were coming.

"Phoenix—come here, child. You have been a blessing to me. Tommy, I was so upset when you and your father fought. I told him he might forbid his daughter from contacting you, but he had no power to tell me what to do.

"I'm so proud of the man you have become and what you have accomplished," the old woman told him.

Tommy interjected, "The letters and pictures you sent me, Grandma, made such a difference. They kept me grounded and allowed me to remain a part of the family and follow Phoenix as she grew. Thank you so much for doing that."

Nodding, their grandmother continued. "Tommy, remember your old teacher, Dr. Johnson, who I found for you to help you understand your gifts?" She saw him nod, and she continued. "As you remember from my letters, Phoenix received a very serious head injury in the same car accident that killed your parents. I have recently contacted Dr. Johnson to work with Phoenix."

"Why?" Tommy asked.

"As a side effect of that injury, she developed the ability to communicate telepathically. Dr. Johnson has been helping her to understand and hone her abilities."

"Phoenix, I'm glad—you are learning from the best. Maybe, in time, we can talk with each other telepathically?" Tommy asked her.

"I sense that you and your sister will be taking different paths after I leave, but I know you will be reunited and will work together in the future."

"I don't have much time left, as the love of my life is impatient for me to join him. I just wanted to tell you how proud your grandparents are of you and how loved you both are."

Closing her eyes for the last time and giving each of her grandchildren's hands a final squeeze, the tiny woman sighed and left them.

Standing at the graveside one last time before they parted, Tommy and Phoenix held hands and realized their grandmother was correct.

After she died, Tommy and Phoenix spent time catching up on the missed years and sharing their dreams for the future. Tommy's plans were to go to New Mexico, where he intended to renovate the old house he inherited from their grandparents and turn it into a motorcycle club for the motorcycle he intended to form with some of his buddies.

Phoenix's path would lead her back to college to complete her degree and graduate.

They both had faith that what their grandmother had told them was true and that they would reunite in the future. This gave them hope and encouragement that, when they parted, it wouldn't be forever.

CHAPTER 1

"Church!" roared the President as the members of the Elemental Spirits filed into the meeting room and took their places around the old oak table. "Oracle has had a vision that will involve one of our family members and the future of the club. It will need to be discussed, decisions made, and voted upon. Oracle, the floor is yours." Roar said as she pounded her gavel.

"Flame, your brother is President of the Mystic Warriors, isn't he?" Oracle asked.

"Yes, his club is in Denton, New Mexico," Flame said. "A few years ago, we inherited property from our grandparents, and Tommy founded his club and located it on his property. Oracle, does your vision involve him and his club?"

"Yes," Oracle said, "the vision I saw had him and his club being attacked by a rival club. If we don't intervene, they may not survive. I saw this outlaw club setting fires and picking off members of his club and innocent people in town in their quest to take over and expand their territory."

"What can we do?" Flame asked. "I know I haven't kept in touch, but I can't lose him. We were "special," and our parents never seemed to understand what we were going through because they didn't have any gifts. Tommy was born with his telepathy and precognition. I had my fire and mind control. Grandma helped me to accept my gifts because she was a Fire mage. She also taught me how to manage my power by remaining calm and concentrating on self-control, so that I didn't harm anyone.

"Grandma was unfamiliar with telepathy but was able to locate someone to help Tommy understand his gifts.

"Tommy and our dad had a major fight while I was still in high school. Tommy left and joined the Army. Dad forbade me to talk or write to him.

"In my freshman year of college, I came home to visit my family over the Thanksgiving holiday. It was during that visit that Mom, Dad, and I were in a very bad car accident, killing my parents and giving me a severe head injury. A side effect of the accident was that I developed telepathy.

"Some of you know this already, but, for those who don't know, it explains why Tommy and this club are so important to me.

"I studied engineering in college and learned hypnotism after attending a magician's show. Once Grandma died and I graduated college, I felt restless. I had no one, so I went in search of other gifted people that I could connect with and feel free to share my powers."

"I bought my bike, made modifications to it, and attached a sidecar. I adopted Woof from the Topeka Humane Society for a companion and protector. His size alone would scare anyone off," Flame grinned.

"Then he and I headed out cross-country looking for like-minded and special people.

"I met Roar outside of Fort Belvoir when I was in Virginia. I had stopped for something to eat, and while waiting for my meal at the outside table, I noticed that she was having a conversation with Woof. His bark and her answer drew my attention, and we started talking. She had just separated from the service and was looking for something herself. We connected right away and agreed to look for others and form a club that was centered around women like us. We and the women we found became close and formed a family. However, the only blood family I have left is Tommy, and, if there is anything I can do to keep him alive, I will do it. I hope my club family will agree to help me in this quest."

"That is what we need to discuss and plan to prevent, Flame," Roar stated.

"Okay. Tommy and I both inherited property from our grandparents. Tommy started his club on his property, while I inherited the adjoining property, where the hotel is located. Even though I haven't done anything with it, we could relocate to Denton and use the hotel as our new clubhouse—if everyone agrees, that is. It probably will need fixing up some, but it's feasible. The problem is that we would also need to re-locate our businesses," explained Flame.

"Rain and Stocks," Roar asked the Treasurer and Business Manager, "is that even possible? Terra? Are you agreeable to moving your pottery business? Windy? Your wind chime shop? And Dex, your construction and design business would be helpful in getting the new clubhouse and new business buildings up and running. That way, we would be onsite when the action starts," suggested Roar.

"Oracle, do you have any idea how much time we have to accomplish the move and get ready for the attack?" Roar asked. "We also would have to go down to Denton and see what shape the hotel is in and what Dex would need to do to get it ready for us to move in. We would need time to scope out the area and find buildings to relocate our businesses. We will also need to meet up with Flame's brother and his club."

"The impression I got was we would have somewhere between four and five months before the gang would make their move on the Warriors. So, everything needs to be in place before that time frame," Oracle informed everyone.

We discussed the logistics, and everyone voiced their opinion and ideas. A vote was taken to relocate to Denton and help the Mystic Warriors.

ONE WEEK LATER

Roar, Dex, and Flame stepped off their bikes. Woof jumped out of the sidecar when Flame released his harness, and they got their first look at Flame's inheritance. Sighing, they saw a dirty-white stucco, three-story Spanish Revival building. The windows were boarded up; the stairway leading to the upper floors and a massive oak door had a rusting iron railing.

"Well, right off the bat, I can see it needs a good cleaning of the stucco and a new coat of whitewash. The tile roof looks okay from down here, but I won't know for sure until I see it from the top. The iron railings will need a good wire-brush cleaning. Absolutely love those oak doors. Can't wait to see what's inside," Dex told Roar and her club mates.

As Flame unlocked the doors and led them into the building, their noses scrunched up at the musty smells of disuse.

"Let's go in and see what we need to change or fix," said Dex as she entered through the large double entrance doors.

Walking the three floors, poking into the foyer, kitchen, bathrooms, offices, bedrooms, and ballroom, Dex opined, "It's doable. On the main floor, we can combine a few offices to make the surgical suite and trauma room. The ballroom will make a great Church and War Room. We can work with the kitchen and dining room, and just update the appliances. The second and third floors can turn into suites with little effort. Let's go check out the basement."

As they reached the bottom of the stairway in the basement and walked around the open area, Flame felt a breeze on her face and attempted to locate the source.

"Hey, look here!" she said excitedly. "There seems to be a door behind this wall of wine. Help me move the rack of bottles. Behold— let there be light!" They looked down a long tunnel before entering and walking down the tiled path. "You know? I think this will lead us to the Warriors compound and maybe even their clubhouse, as it seems to lead in that direction," Flame speculated. "Should we check it out?"

"Hell, yeah, Flame," Roar said eagerly. "We might find it useful if we need to escape or even transport supplies between the two clubs. Let's make sure to see what condition it's in and confirm where it goes."

Walking the length of the tunnel, the three women used their phones to light the path and indeed, came upon a door. It was locked, but the location told them that it should lead to the Warriors basement. "You know?" Flame says, "Grandma told me stories about Prohibition and how bootleggers transported liquor across the border and hid it in tunnels. I bet these were some of the ones she was talking about."

Finishing the tour, the women discussed what they found and what needed to be accomplished in the time remaining. "I'll get my crew right on it; we should be able to move in by the end of the month," Dex told us.

"On the whole, it's not in bad shape. The roof tiles looked intact. It shouldn't take much to clean up the exterior. Inside, a deep clean will be necessary after we rearrange a few walls; that will help make it ready to set up the trauma and surgical suites. Then it's a matter of decorating the individual suites and bedrooms and putting in the game room. All the kitchen needs are new appliances, and the place will be ready to move in once our stuff from the old clubhouse arrives.

"The others will also be able to move their businesses here within the next month and a half, so that timeline will work well," Dex told them.

"Okay. Let's get back to the club. Dex, you get your crew started; everyone else will finish packing up and moving," Roar instructed. "Flame, you go see and talk with your brother, and we'll meet with you once that's done."

"I think that would be best. I'll let them know what Oracle saw in her vision," Flame responded. "I can then tell Tommy our plans about the hotel and suggest ways that our club can assist them."

Looking impressive geared up in the special helmet and goggles Flame fabricated for him, Woof eagerly settled into the sidecar, and they took off for the short ride next door to the Warriors' compound.

At the gate was a man wearing a leather vest, or cut, that showed his name, "Cyclone," on the left chest patch and his title, "Prospect," on the right patch. Practicing a little mind control, Flame suggested he open the gates and allow Woof and her to enter. Flame pulled up in front of the clubhouse, removed the helmets that she and her dog were wearing and walked to the door of the room, guarded by another Prospect. She told him to open the door and allow Woof and her to enter. They entered what she assumed to be the sacred conference room, or Church, and a powerful male voice slammed into Flame, that caused her to stop momentarily in her tracks, but she recovered quickly.

"What the hell are you doing here?" boomed the Warriors' President in a deep bass.

"Hello, brother dear. Long time no see," Flame informed him and the room filled with 20 large men.

Woof bared his teeth; the hackles rose on his back, and he took a protective stance in front of Flame. She lowered herself into a chair and placed a hand on Woof's head to calm him. As the volume from the angry men's voices decreased, she looked into the grim and stormy hazel-gray eyes of her brother, telling him how she was now going by "Flame." Before her, was a tall, auburn-haired, well-muscled, tattooed man that she hadn't seen since their grandmother's funeral. Getting straight to the point, she asked, "Do you know who the Satan's Spawn are?"

"Some 1% MC west of here," he growled.

"Do you also know they have plans for killing all of you and taking over everything you own, including this compound?"

Again, the room erupted in the sound of angry men swearing, yelling, and beating their fists on the table. Woof added his voice to the cacophony. "Where did you learn this?" they shouted at me from all directions.

Showing no fear, Flame told the room,"If you shut up and listen, you will find out." Her brother then stood up and banged his gavel for quiet, and silence filled the room once more.

"Our psychic advisor, Oracle, had a vision a week ago about you and this club being in danger unless we joined our clubs and defended each other. Because if we didn't, the Mystic Warriors wouldn't have enough resources to defend yourselves. We have made plans to relocate and join forces to protect the clubs, using the strengths and gifts of each member.

"If your compound is endangered, so is our new clubhouse, which is the hotel next door. Did you know there's a secret tunnel connecting both properties? No? There is. It's in the hotel basement behind a wine rack and runs underground until connecting to the basement in your clubhouse. We found it when we toured the hotel.

"You don't know me or my club, the Elemental Spirits. I need to share things we usually don't speak of with others. As the name implies, our gifts involve nature's powers, or, as we call them, Gifts. We have members who control water, wind, the earth, and fire. We also have gifts of telepathy, precognition, dream travel, and mind control. One of our sisters can speak with animals. I can't tell you all the gifts because they are evolving as new members join our club. I can tell you that I am a Fire mage and have the gift of telepathy and mind control, so don't punish the Prospects, as I made them do what they normally wouldn't have done by opening the gates and door for me.

"Some of us have served our country in the military and can handle weapons and explosives, and expertly engage in hand-to-hand combat. We have been trained to fix and maintain anything with two or more wheels. Another important thing to mention is that our doctor heals with both conventional medicine and touch."

"This is what we can bring to the table, brother. What can your men do?" she inquired as she ended my rapid-fire explanations.

As Seer looked at the shocked expressions of the men surrounding him and he said to himself, "I wasn't aware of another club that had the same gifts as we do.

"As you know, Flame, I am telepathic and have precognition instead of Fire. My club members have similar gifts to your club. Torch is the one that shares your gift. Others in this room have the control of storms, electricity, telekinesis, and earth elements. They, too, have served our country in the military as I have. I go by Seer now," he explained in a voice that grew stronger as he talked.

"Our contractor thinks we will be able to move into the hotel by the end of the month," Flame notified them. "At that time, my President, Roar, will want you and some of your men to meet us at the hotel to discuss and plan our strategy. We can do a meet-and-greet and see what security we need to beef up for both compounds and the businesses. I'll let you know when we are ready for that meeting. Okay, let's get this show on the road, as time is running out. See you in two to three weeks." With that, Woof and Flame stood and walked out of the room to head back home to their old clubhouse in Taos.

CHAPTER 2

"Wow! What a hot piece that was," Torch mumbled under his breath. "Why haven't you told us you had such a hot sister?" as he remembered the red-headed Amazon who had strode confidently into a room full of bikers.

"Phoenix, aka Flame, was in college when she and our parents were in an accident, injuring Flame and killing our parents."

"I was away on a mission, so Flame and Grandma had to deal with not only their deaths but the estate as well. Thank goodness Grandma was there to help."

"So, when our grandma died, I was able to be with my sister and help her settle Grandma's estate, but that was the last time I saw or spoke with her.

"I moved to New Mexico and started our club. Phoenix finished the last three years of her engineering degree and then dropped off the map. I'm not sure where she went or what she did."

"How do you and everyone else feel about her club?" Mountain asked. "I, for one, am curious."

"I'm as shocked as most of you are," Seer told the room.

"Wire? No scuttlebutt on the dark web about this MC or their plans? We need more intel before that meeting, so we don't look any more like idiots than we do now. How did I not pick up on this?" grumbled Seer to himself.

"On it." Wire sprinted from the room, heading to the secure room lined with monitors, keyboards, and servers—anything and everything a geek could want.

"Mountain, I want you and Torch to work on locating any weakness in the perimeter that needs to be shored up, as well as the businesses. I also want you to locate that tunnel Flame said they found in our basement and work with Wire on the security and how we can integrate with the women's systems.

"Torch, I want you to be the one working closely with Flame.

"Doc, make sure the infirmary is set for triage and extra supplies laid in. Get with Flame's club doctor, and see what they have set up."

Pulling the Prospect Groundhog from guarding the room, Seer ordered him to scope out the dirtbags Satan's Spawn and bring back any intel he can dig up. "Tell Cyclone he will be on gate duty; be extra vigilant and report any activity or suspicious goings-on.

"I'll work with their President, and we will oversee the brothers and sisters. Okay, get moving, and find out as much as you can," Seer said, finishing up delegating tasks.

Flame stopped in La Joya to rest and grab a few hours of sleep. It had been a long ride and meeting her brother had been stressful, so Flame needed the down time before finishing the journey and reporting on how things had gone at her brother's compound.

The next morning, she informed the Elemental Spirits that Seer had dropped a bomb, saying his club had far more gifted members than she realized! Flame always knew that her brother had talents, but didn't realized his men might have them also. That would make things even more interesting when Satan's Spawn make their play.

She wondered if the six-foot-plus dark auburn-haired Torch lived up to his name and how hot an inferno would be ignited when two fires join. Her mind raced between Torch and her brother Seer's club members, what gifts they had, and how we could use those gifts to protect the clubs and destroy Satan's Spawn. The Mystic Warriors would meet with the Elemental Spirits in two or three weeks to make plans and compare their strengths and weaknesses for ways to improve their defenses.

One Month Later

The last of Flame's equipment was finally loaded on the trailer, and she was on her way to join the rest of the club. Fifty miles outside of Denton, She heard a *Pop!* and the trailer started to sway and then thump, thump, thump. "Shit! That's all I need—a flat!" She pulled to the side of the road, surveyed the damage; the trailer's left rear tire was as flat as a pancake. "Guess I have to pull up my big-girl panties," Flame told Woof. She removed the spare from the truck and got to work changing the tire. "I'll stop at the first garage and get a new tire or have this one repaired," as she continued muttering while she replaced the flattened tire. "Okay, Woof—let's hit the road and look for that garage."

She spied a sign saying, **"JOE'S GARAGE AND TIRE SHOP Next Right."** *Great! As soon as I get this tire situation out of the way,* *we can get back on the road and meet up with the rest of my club,"* she thought. Over the past month, Dex and her crew had worked nonstop in preparation for the relocation to Denton and the move to the hotel, which they had christened "The Clubhouse."

As Flame arrived at Joe's Garage in Rockfield, she saw two men lounging outside the side entrance of the office. She didn't like the looks of them, and neither did Woof, as he softly growled.

She told Woof, "It's okay, boy. I don't like them either." They were rough, unkempt, and gave off some really bad vibes. Their cuts said *Satan's Spawn.*

Parking her rig, she walked around behind the bay doors and overheard them talking. The blond-haired, tall guy grumbled, "Can't wait until we wipe out those Warriors. They have some sweet moneymakers we can offload easily."

Short Beer Belly jumped in with, "Yeah, Rat says we can start moving in as soon as the last of our shipments we have lined up are delivered."

Carefully so they didn't see or hear her, she made her way back to the front office and bought a new tire for the trailer. She had to get to the club and tell them what she'd learned before she called her brother.

She realized shit may be hitting the fan sooner than everyone thought.

That Night

After Flame spoke with Roar, she called her brother. "Seer, on my way to town, I had a flat tire. The garage I stopped at to repair it had a couple of the Satan's Spawn hanging out. I overheard them talking that as soon as some shipments they have in progress are delivered, Rat, their President, wants to start moving on Denton and the Warriors.

"Roar, my President, would like you and your men to meet with us at 9 a.m. tomorrow for that meet-and-greet I mentioned," Flame notified Seer.

"We will be there," Seer told her.

After the call disconnected, Seer bellowed, "Torch, Mountain, Wire, my office. Now!" As the men took their places, he informed them that the President of the Elemental Spirits wants to meet with them at 9 in the morning. "I want all of you to go with me. Be ready."

The Following Morning

As they gazed at the impressive three-story building in front of them, Seer, Torch, Mountain, and Wire took in the number of windows, doors, and defensible space surrounding the perimeter, outlying buildings, and garages. "Going to be a bitch to defend," the seven-foot-tall giant of a man grunted in a deep voice. "They don't even have fences, walls, or gates that can be closed off. Besides the tunnel, maybe we should put in gates, allowing access between the two properties," Mountain mused.

"I see satellite dishes mounted on the roofs. I'll have to get with their IT person and check on their servers and encryption," Wire said, considering the logistics.

"Come on, brothers. We've wasted enough time outside. Let's go meet our counterparts and exchange intel so we can formulate plans on how to proceed," Seer said thoughtfully.

"Welcome, gentlemen, to our Clubhouse. My name is Roar, and I'm the President of the Elemental Spirits," the tall, tawny-haired woman with amber eyes said as she opened the strong oak doors. "Come in, and I'll show you to our Church and War Room. It was once a ballroom and can hold more than 200 people, so it should fit our needs. Please sit down, and let's introduce ourselves. Flame told us your club has gifts, like ours. As you meet us, we'll tell you about our gifts, as I hope you and your men will do when they introduce themselves.

"I was in Army Intelligence, and I can speak, write, read, and understand any language I hear and do it as well as a native. I am also telepathic and able to speak with animals.

"You have met my VP, Flame.

"I will have my Officers introduce themselves and explain their roles and gifts. Let's start with our Enforcer, Windy."

Watching the men alertly, the tall, flaxen-haired woman nodded. "I am a Wind and Storm mage. I'm able to brew up storms, and control winds and lightning. I also have earned a black belt in Krav Maga."

As she raised her hand, the tall, dark woman on Windy's right said, "I'm Ink, the club Secretary. I have a photographic memory and can reproduce anything I see, including different handwriting and signatures, which makes me an expert forger."

"My name is Stocks, and I'm our club Treasurer. I can take care of or manipulate anything involving numbers," said the tall blonde.

"I'm a Water mage, so I control water from the sky, rivers, seas—even the water in your drinking glass," said the woman with the purple streak in her blond hair.

"Rain is also our Business Manager," Roar interjected.

"Patch is our doctor. She can heal by touch or with conventional medicine. She is also our surgeon." Roar pointed to the blonde on Windy's left.

"I'm Ghost. I will be paired with your IT specialist, as I can infiltrate the Web and follow trails from computers to any source without being detected. I will be responsible for monitoring security cameras from the businesses. As Oracle and I are the two shortest members of the club, we are sometimes jokingly referred to as 'Sprites.'"

"Terra is the woman standing by the door," Roar said as she started her final introduction. "She has gifts that involve the earth elements—soil, rocks, and even the dust in the air. Although she is still a Prospect, we value her place in our club.

"This is the core, except for Oracle, who was the one that had the vision sending us here, and Dex, our construction engineer and Earth mage."

Seer, Torch, and the other men exchanged glances, and unspoken messages flashed between them, until Seer opened his mouth and voiced the decisions to be made.

"Thank you, Roar, for the introductions and sharing your clubs' gifts with us. Yes, some of my club brothers share the same gifts, and, we agree that, by joining together, we will be stronger.

"We will start introducing ourselves. Then we can share what we know, what we need to do, and how we will go about protecting ourselves. Is that agreeable to you?" inquired Seer.

All heads nodded, Seer began to introduce himself. "My name is Thomas "Seer" O'Donnell," said the tall, auburn-haired President of the Mystic Warriors. "I am an explosives expert, ex-Army Ranger, Flame's brother, and, occasionally, able to see the future in my dreams."

The 6'3", blue-eyed man raised his hand. "I'm Quinn "Torch" O'Shay. I am VP of the Mystic Warriors. Seer and I served together in the Rangers. I, like Flame, can handle and control fire, and I'm also telepathic."

Next a very large, tall man introduced himself. "I am the Enforcer of our club, William "Mountain" Wilcox. I was a construction engineer in the Navy and can build or tear down anything that man might make from any materials found on Earth. My gifts and talents sound like Terra's and Dex's, so my hope is that we can work together to construct defensive walls."

As he smiled at Ghost, a man who had been pacing around the room started speaking. "My name is Jack 'Wire' Harris, IT specialist and an Electrical mage who will be working with you on communication, intel gathering, and the security cameras."

"Seer, Roar—a rapid-response team will need to be formed to be on call in case those panic buttons are activated and also for any other emergencies that might arise," Flame added.

"I can work on that," Roar said. "I'll pull from both clubs and see if there are enough to form two teams."

"Doc couldn't join us this morning, as he is securing supplies and making sure the trauma room and equipment are available, but his gifts are similar to your doctor's and will be getting together with her later," Seer informed them.

After all the introductions, they started pulling up blueprints on the buildings and going over what would be needed to quickly shore up the defenses—to shift from a defensive to offensive position—and what supplies will be needed.

"Roar, when you were revamping the hotel, did you designate a room for a clinic or trauma room?" asked Seer.

"Yes, we also have a small operating room adjacent to the clinic area. Patch can work closely with Doc to see what will be needed to fully cover those areas. One of our members was also a combat nurse, so she can help staff the OR and trauma rooms. Do you have anyone who can split shifts with her?" Roar inquired.

"Yes, one of our brothers was a corpsman in the Navy, and he also has a healing touch, so he can work with your nurse, and we have a Prospect who was a para-rescue in the Air Force," Seer responded.

"How big is the connecting tunnel?" Seer asked. Is it strong enough to run an ATV to transport patients or supplies?"

Wheels started turning in Roar's head as she thought the question over. "Yes, I think that would work. Terra and Mountain may have to tweak a few things, but yes, it's feasible."

As he bent over the blueprints for both clubs Mountain placed his big finger where the tunnel between the clubs should be but couldn't locate it. "Everyone, I want your attention here. This is where the tunnel should be, however, it doesn't appear on either of our blueprints. This could be either because it was built after the prints were made or that because whoever built our buildings didn't want anyone to know it existed."

"When I was down in the tunnel earlier," Mountain continued, "I found some places where other tunnels branched off the main shaft. I haven't had a chance yet to explore them, as we're concentrating on the current threat, but we will need to explore them once this situation is resolved. We might be able to utilize them in the future.

"Right now, we're working to get electricity down there so we can run lights."

"Makes sense, Mountain," Seer told the mage. "Are you confident they don't present any danger to us now? Are they something we can afford to put on the back burner?"

"Yes, I blocked them and made sure they can't open or be used until we want them and have time to see where they lead," answered Mountain.

Having heard that, at the back of all our minds was the knowledge that time was flying by, and the pressure to complete everything before the Spawn made their first moves weighed heavy on everyone.

CHAPTER 3

"Groundhog report!" Sitting together in the War Room at the Hotel, everyone from both clubs was listening intently to the information gleaned by the Warriors' Prospect.

"Seems like Satan's Spawn is based out of Lordsburg. It's a 1% club that runs illegals across the border—also guns, liquor, and drugs. There are around 30 in their club, led by their President Rat, a smelly, lowlife bastard. Rumor has it he backstabbed his way to the top and finally was made President when the old one just happened to disappear after a night of drinking with Rat," explained Groundhog.

"Word is Rat is hungry to expand his territory and open new trade routes; he has his heart set on taking over ours. He has loaded trucks headed to El Paso now, and, as soon as they are delivered and offloaded and his other orders delivered, he plans on setting his sights on Denton and our club.

"Way I figure it, we have two or three weeks before we start seeing how the Spawn plan to carry out Rat's orders," finished Groundhog.

"Mountain, what progress are you and Terra making on the main tunnel?" asked Seer.

The large man responded, "We built some niches where we can stash guns, ammunition, and other equipment in case we need a quick grab.

Seer continued, "Roar—any thoughts on what else we need? Can you get the quick-response teams together and see about installing panic buttons with Wire and Ghost?"

"Yes, the response teams are ready, but we still need to install the panic buttons," Roar answered.

"I know it's a hell of a lot to do and ask of everyone in such a short time. What are your thoughts about pulling in other clubs to help?" asked Torch.

"If your allies have heavy equipment and operators they can spare, it will take some of the pressure off us, and we could put up different crews for the businesses and compounds," mused Roar.

"Good idea—let me place a few calls and see if I can call in a few markers." Seer grabbed his phone and stalked off.

Torch looked at Flame and grabbed her hand without warning—it surprised Flame that he could touch her without being harmed. They walked out the doors to exit the room. "With both of us being able to control fire, how do you suggest we use it?" questioned Torch.

"I've never had to use my gifts in combat. I'm at a loss here, so any ideas would help. I can read minds, but I would need to be close," Flame told Torch, still dazed at being able to hold his strong hand.

"Okay, let's make Molotov cocktails the others can use if we aren't around. We'll gather bottles and other supplies and make enough cocktails that we can divide the stash and store some at each compound. That way, not only we but other brothers or sisters can use them if needed. We will also have to be alert for any fires that the Spawn might set and be ready to put them out as quickly as possible. So, in addition to collecting the bottles, we will need to get fire extinguishers and stash them in both compounds," Torch suggested.

"Let's go see if Wire and Ghost need us to set any cameras while we're in town collecting supplies. We are going to have to split up to cover the different areas and businesses if there is any hope of getting everything set up and running in time," Torch said. "Do you know how to wire the cameras and panic buttons?"

"Yes, I can handle that," I responded.

As they walked past the hotel, they saw Dex's crew placing the heavy blocks forming the walls that would span the front of the hotel and act as the first line of defense. The heavy iron gates and security shack would be added later, along with communications connecting them to the clubhouses, for when the other construction teams arrive with more equipment.

"Looks like things are starting to take shape. I just hope we have time to complete everything before the shit hits the fan. Has Oracle had any other visions?" asked Torch.

"She had been getting flashes—nothing detailed enough that it would help—but she says she will keep trying. Has Seer received anything? I know he sometimes has precognitive dreams, and I know he was upset that he was blindsided about Rat's plans," Flame said.

"No, nothing that he has shared," Torch mumbled.

Entering the Warriors' clubhouse, we were surrounded by a hive of activity: boxes being moved in and out of storage, shelves being stocked, phones ringing, raised voices calling out orders.

Placing his hand on Flame's back, Torch guided her to the room Wire had set up. Monitors showed views of the exterior of both compounds; other monitors showed the front and back doors and alleys behind both clubs' businesses and the side entrances. Ghost was threading her way through the dark web, trying to capture any whispers that might reveal what the Spawn were up to.

"Hate to disturb you guys," interrupted Torch, "but we're on our way to town to pick up supplies and thought you might want us to set cameras up inside the buildings or help Roar set up panic buttons."

Looking at Ghost, Wire asked, "You guys have extra cameras we can use?"

"We stopped off on the way here and bought a whole crapload of home security systems we can use. They're low-tech but should work. We also have some electronics that we can adapt for the panic buttons. We would need to dedicate a monitor solely for the panic buttons, so we can zoom in—in real time—to whatever is happening," Ghost informed them. "If you can set the inside systems and the panic buttons, then we can test them and their placement, and adjust if needed. Just let Roar know that you will be setting up the panic buttons."

As Torch and Flame left the Warriors' clubhouse, they decided to take Torch's truck. They loaded up the back with the cameras, electronics, and tools needed to mount them. When they returned, they had the supplies to make our Molotov cocktails and the fire extinguishers.

Arriving at the Mystic Warriors Pawnshop, Torch pulled into a parking space, got out, and walked to the back of the truck. "Flame, if you can place the cameras over the doorways facing into the rooms,

I'll work on putting the panic buttons in the offices. We've already had some security measures in here, so we are basically fine-tuning them. If you need a stepstool to reach anything, let me know," Torch said, looking her way.

At six feet tall, Flame can reach most things, but she grinned and thanked Torch for trying to make things easier for her, and got to work.

CHAPTER 4

After finishing the pawn shop, Torch and Flame moved on to Terra's pottery shop, followed by Windy's place, the tattoo parlor and garage that the Warriors operated, and then we decided to break for lunch.

As Torch looked into Flame's green eyes, passed her a napkin, and their hands touched, heat rushed from his fingers up her arm reinforcing the knowledge that fire burns in both their souls. Flame's eyes widened as she also realized how combustible they could be together.

"Torch? I know you felt that, too. I don't know why I didn't feel that spark when I held your hand earlier, but now that I have, I want to explore it with you," Flame whispered, I want to get to know you better—but not just because we both share the power of fire. I have never met anyone that had the same gifts that I have, so I've had to be extremely careful when touching anyone. I also know this isn't really the time, with everything going down, but I don't want to lose this feeling of being able to touch someone without the fear that I would hurt them," she sighed in amazement.

"I feel the same, Flame. I've never been able to relax my guard and really touch someone without that same fear of hurting them. When we held hands earlier, I did it without thinking; it just felt right, and it caught me unprepared. But with you sharing the same gift, I think it might be the reason we can touch without harming each other. I agree this really isn't the best time but would like to spend as much time as possible with you," Torch responded.

"I can't promise you I won't get hurt, but I will try my damnedest to survive and protect you." Torch reached for Flame's hand, and the warmth of his touch returned—warm and caring but without the fear of hurting each other.

"As much as I want to continue this conversation, we have a lot to do, and time is running out. Maybe tonight we can discuss this subject further," Torch grinned.

A wide smile appeared on Flame's face as Torch paid for their lunch, and they headed out to finish setting up the cameras and panic buttons in the remaining businesses before collecting the bottles, fuel, and wicks for the Molotov cocktails as well as additional fire extinguishers. The pair then returned to the compounds to start making the firebombs and placing the extinguishers.

After that task was finished they headed over to the Mystic Warriors' dining room for dinner and joined the other club members. Conversation ranged from what everyone had worked on during the day to what still needed to be done or finished. The groups laughed, talked, drank, got to know each other, and shared their gifts while playing pool and darts.

After dinner and shared time with other club members, Torch and Flame walked over to the hotel. During the day, a gate had been put in, that allowed the clubs to cut across the grounds for quicker access than having to take the road. Now there were two ways—the tunnel and the gates that connected the properties.

Flame opened the door to her suite, and Woof jumped up off the sofa and greeted them. She laughed as she told Torch, "We need to take this big guy out for a run and to do his business. He's been cooped up most of the day and really needs to get some exercise. Flame grabbed Woof's leash, then they headed back outside, holding hands.

While they walked around the grounds as Woof explored, Flame and Torch picked up the conversation they had started at lunch.

"Torch, tell me about yourself. I know only what you told everyone when we introduced our clubs. Can you tell me more?" Flame asked him.

"Where should I start?" asked Torch.

"Anywhere you'd like," she responded.

"Okay. I'm 29 years old. Middle child, with two older brothers and a younger sister. My father was a Fire Chief, and my mom was a nurse in a burn unit. Both my older brothers were Hot Shot firefighters for the forest service. They jump from planes and fight fires in remote areas. My baby sister is an arson specialist. We all control fire in our own ways, but I'm the one that actually *controls* fire.

"I met your brother in the Army and went through Ranger training together. Over the years, we learned about each other's gifts and those of our commanding officer and other team members. How our unit got together, I'm not sure, but when Seer decided to form the club and invited me, I jumped at the chance, and here we are.

"Now it's your turn, Flame. Tell me about yourself," inquired Torch.

She gazed over at her dog as he sniffed the bushes and trees. Memories flooded her mind and Flame slipped into the past. "It was just Mom, Dad, Tommy, me, and our grandparents in this big old monstrosity of a house. Grandma and Grandpa were special and had gifts like we do, but Mom and Dad had trouble accepting what we could do and clashed with us frequently.

"Then Grandpa died, and Dad got worse. Nothing Tommy or I did was right. When Dad and Tommy had their blow-up fight about Tommy joining the Army, my life changed.

"Tommy wasn't there to act as a buffer, so all the insults about being a *fire starter* like our grandparents came at Grandma and me full force."

"Mom was under Dad's thumb and was not much help. It was such a relief when I left for college. I came home only because of Grandma. That was why I was there the weekend of the accident."

"Dad was complaining about something and not paying attention to his driving when the crash happened, killing both my parents. They had to use the 'jaws of life' to extract me from the car.

"Grandma was there for me and helped me make all the decisions about the funerals and estate. She arranged for me to study with Tommy's teacher when my telepathy made an appearance."

"Then, when Grandma became ill, she was able to contact my brother in a dream. He arrived just before she died. I went back to finish college, and Tommy came here.

"I graduated and traveled around freelancing as a motorcycle fabricator until meeting up with Roar and building our club. That's it in a nutshell."

"Now, I think Woof is finished, so how about going inside?" she suggested.

When they returned to the suite, Touch pinned Flame against the door, and his lips were against hers. It was hot, wet, and wild.

Coming up for air, Flame opened her eyes wide and gazed at Torch. "Wow! Guess that answers the question about being able to touch you. I must tell you, this is all new to me. Fear of setting someone on fire has kept me from touching anyone, much less being intimate. I haven't had any experience in making love or being loved by anyone. I learned how to control my gift, but I have not allowed anyone to get close," she told him.

"Torch, I want you with every fiber of my being, but I'm scared. We've only just met. We've been able to touch, but I don't know what will happen if we go further," Flame confessed.

"I don't want to disappoint you or myself by not knowing what to do or how to please you. I know that, when you touch me, it excites me, and I want more. I want to feel your hands and lips on me. I want to become one with you in every sense of the word."

As he took her face in his hands and looked intently into her green eyes, Torch said, "Yes, we've just met, but I have never been drawn to a person before or felt what I am feeling for you with anyone in my life. I realize what you are telling me. We can take things as slow as you want, and, if there's any sign that either of us is starting to smoke, we'll stop," he grinned.

"I do take this seriously, and I'm so honored I will be your first lover. I'm not afraid of you, and I know if we both survived those kisses, as hot as they were, we will survive making love. I feel it in my bones, in my heart, and in the fire that burns within me. This will last a lifetime. Your fire draws me to you and kindles my fire to blend with yours and grow. I truly believe your fire will never harm me, as mine will not hurt you," Torch reassured her.

"When we are together, I want you to call me by my given name, 'Quinn,' not my road name."

"But you must call me 'Phoenix' as well. Can we try those kisses again?"

"Oh, yes. I think we should try those kisses again," he growled, and drew her into his arms.

The Next Morning

Just as the sun filtered through the curtains, she opened her eyes and felt a strong arm lying across her stomach and a warm breath on her neck. Smiling, Flame remembered how the night passed, with wonder. She thought about how patient and gentle he was with her, and gazed down at his sculptured, firm, muscular body. She realized, *This man is mine.* She noticed a change in Quinn's breathing. As he rolled over onto his back, she gazed on the smiling face of her lover, her man.

"Good morning, sunshine," his gravely baritone voice said. "You been up long? How are you feeling?"

"Wonderful," Flame grinned. "I'm amazed that we both survived, and I can lay aside all my fears of touching you," Flame laughed.

Torch chuckled and said, "Right now, we need to shower, report for duty, and see what else needs to be done," he reminded her.

"Yes, playtime is over for now. Race you to the shower." Flame threw off the covers, dashed to the bathroom and turned on the water. As he caught up with her, Quinn placed a deep, hot kiss on her lips.

All too soon, the water cooled reminded them that they had places they needed to be and important things to do.

CHAPTER 5

While they sat at the head of the long table made from Spanish oak, Seer and Rage called the meeting to order.

"Report!" Seer barked. "Dex, how are the walls and security shack coming along?"

"Walls are up, thanks to the hard work of my crew and the extra hands and equipment supplied by the Silver City Kings and everyone putting in extra hours working late. The front gate should be installed by tomorrow afternoon, along with the security shack and communication to the clubhouses. The gate allowing access to both places went in yesterday morning."

"Thank you, Dex, and thank you to the crews for their hard work," praised Seer and Roar.

"How about the cameras and panic buttons? Ghost, were you and Wire able to integrate both systems? Anything popping up on the dark web about these scumbags?" inquired Seer.

"Yes, Wire and I were able to sync both systems, and, with our own servers in place, no one can hack into them. The exterior cameras on the buildings are up and running. We have clear views of not only the businesses but also the streets in front, the alleys behind, and the side entrances, too," Ghost briefed everyone. She added, "I haven't been able to find any intel about the Spawn that relates to the clubs, but I'll keep checking and let you know if and when I pick anything up."

Wire jumped in and said, "Torch and Flame installed the interior cameras and panic buttons yesterday, and we have fine-tuned their placement, so every room is covered. We have added a monitor set exclusively for the panic buttons to allow us real-time coverage and recordings."

"We have also set up a satellite room in the hotel so we can monitor from both locations," said Ghost.

"Excellent work," Seer said as he looked over to Roar. "Have you set up the rapid-response team?"

"Yes, there is a roster listing everyone's name and which team they are on. Since some of your men and my sisters have the same skills, I was able to make two complete teams. We should be able to cover the four elements of wind, water, fire, and anything involving the earth, and hit them with things they are not aware we have. Conveniently, we can also hit them with the ordinances and guns we both must draw on," Roar said.

"Doc, were you and Patch and the nurses able to equip and stock the trauma clinic and OR?" Seer asked.

"Yes, both camps are set up for any contingency we can think of. Supplies are stocked and ready. We also have shift rotations set up subject to change with the situation.

"We also went through the tunnel with Mountain and Terra, and it's tall and wide enough for ATVs and transport gurneys. Good thing both buildings have elevators from the basement and wine cellar: that will allow us to bring patients up to the medical rooms from the tunnel. However, the problem is getting the ATVs down there," reported Doc.

"While we were in the tunnel, Mountain identified niches to store ordinances, guns, and ammo. It's just a matter of stocking them and maybe adding some medical supplies," Patch informed them.

Spokes, chief mechanic at the Mystic Warrior Garage, jumped in. "The other mechanics and I looked to see if the ATVs will fit into the elevators, and, if they won't, we can take them apart and reassemble them in the tunnels, if needed."

"Great idea!" said Roar.

"Okay, now how are we stocked for food and drink? Who will be doing the cooking? Do we have anyone responsible for that?" Seer asked.

"Prez, I know the Prospects have been doing the meals all this time and it isn't a good time to bring anyone new in, but I served with a guy who is a whiz in the kitchen. He is also a Le Cordon Bleu chef," Spokes piped up. " He just retired and was asking me about the club. I'm sure I can get him on-board if everyone agrees."

Seer looked around the room and saw everyone's wide grins. He told Spokes to give the guy a call and see if he would come, and to ask him if he knows anyone else he can work with in the kitchen.

"So, have we covered all the bases?" Seer asked the group. "Any resources we need to deploy? Anyone think of anything we missed? No? Then we need to turn our thoughts from defending ourselves to how are we going to kick these a-holes out of our town and territory.

"Think on it, and we will re-convene at 8 a.m."

"Church adjourned."

CHAPTER 6

After Church, everyone walked into the common room. They grabbed a drink from the bar, sat at a table, or moved toward the dartboard and pool-tables. The men and women of the two clubs tossed ideas around. Laughter broke out here and there as jokes were told to relieve the tension—that was as thick and heavy as fog over the river in winter.

The hours passed slowly, and couples started peeling off, said goodnight and entered their rooms. All that was left were the single, unattached ones to continue drinking or playing games.

Torch looked at Flame and suggested they head to their room at the hotel. Nodding, Flame set her glass down and hopped off the barstool. She said goodnight to her brother and kissed his cheek, as she nodded her head at Roar. They walked across the grounds. "We need to let Woof out to run and relieve himself—we haven't spent much time with him lately. We are a package deal," Flame snickered.

Chuckling, Quinn teased, "You know, he scared the shit out of me when you brought him with you that first night and he started growling. When his hackles went up, I swear he grew to twice his original size, and he's a big, big dog to begin with."

"Yeah, he is my big protector," Flame giggled. "He really is a marshmallow once he gets to know you."

"Once we see to his needs, I'm going to take you to bed and make love to my woman and see to her needs," Quinn vowed. "I'm feeling in my bones that things are going to start soon, and I want to spend as much time as possible with the woman I've come to love."

As she threw her arms around Torch's neck, Flame laid a blistering kiss on his lips and softly told him she loved him, too. "Let's get Woof taken care of, and I'll show you."

Seer fell into a deep but troubled sleep. Worries about the upcoming conflict bombarded him from every side. Had he done enough to protect his club brothers and his sisters' club? Had he forgotten anything? Was anything important left undone?

As he tossed and turned, a smirking face appeared before him. Dark, greasy hair and long shaggy beard, tattoos of devil's heads, and babies with horns covered the arms of this evil man. "I'm coming for you," he spat out from a mouth filled with yellowing and missing teeth. As quickly as that scene appeared, another one took its place. This time it was a large warehouse filled with men, as filthy as the first one, sitting around drinking. Listening hard, Seer heard them crowing about how they were going to bring him and his club down.

"We'll start by ripping off the places on the east side and smashing their businesses and setting fire to them," their leader slurred. "They won't expect us to come from that direction. While they're busy trying to put out the fires and save their businesses, we'll hit their clubhouse. Kill anyone that tries to stop us. Once we rid the town of the Warriors, we'll take over," he laughed hysterically. "Make sure your weapons are cleaned and loaded, and bikes gassed up. We will ride in two days."

Jerked awake in a cold sweat with his wet sheets wrapped tightly around him, Seer now knew what he had to do.

Come morning, the Warriors and Spirits would set their own plans in motion.

CHAPTER 7

Jolted awake, Flame sat up in bed in her suite at the hotel, the feeling that her brother Tommy, aka Seer, was in distress grabbed at her heart. Having worked with other in the Elemental Spirits who were telepathic, she now was able to use that gift received at the time of her head injury, As she reached out with her mind, Flame sent a message to Seer. "Tommy, are you all right? I feel something is wrong."

"I'm okay—just had one of my dreams," Tommy reported. "I'll tell you and everyone else all about it this morning when we meet. Can you ask if Oracle has had any visions? I would really like to discuss my dream with her before the meeting."

"Sure thing. Is there anything else I can help you with?" Flame asked.

"No, not right now. I'll see you soon. You do know I love you, sis, don't you? We haven't seen or spoken much, but that hasn't changed my love for you."

"I know, Tommy, and I love you, too. Don't let anything bad happen to you. I have only one brother, and I don't want to lose him.

It was horrible when Dad ordered me not to have anything to do with you. Then, when the folks died in the car accident, I felt so alone. If it hadn't been for Grandma, I don't know what I would have done. She was the one who taught me how to control my gift of fire. I guess it must have skipped a generation, because I never heard Mom—or Grandma—say anything about them having any gifts. When you were on missions, I couldn't reach you because I hadn't learned how to use my telepathy."

"I hear you, sis. It wasn't easy for me, either, and I regret not being there for you. But I'm glad you're here now. You take care, too, and I'll meet up with you later," he declared as we disconnected.

Flame met Quinn's eyes as he watched her. "Honey, were you just talking with your brother?"

"Yes, I woke up feeling something was wrong with him. I just needed to reassure myself he was okay, so I reached out to him. He wants me to check with Oracle to see if she has had any more visions. He had one of his dreams tonight and wants to meet with her before everyone gets together and compare what each has seen."

"Well, why don't we take care of Woof, talk to Oracle and then find some breakfast before Church. Sound good?" he asked.

"Sounds good. I have a feeling I won't feel much like eating after we hear what he dreamed," Flame said.

LATER THAT MORNING

Everyone filed into the War Room at the hotel, "Good thing this is such a large room, or else not everyone would fit," noticed Mountain. "Our Church wouldn't be able to hold both clubs comfortably."

As they took their places around the room, the sound quieted down, and all eyes turned expectantly to the front, where Seer stood. The group held their breath as they wondered what he would tell them.

"Come to order," Seer yelled as he hammered on the table. "I want to introduce Oracle to those of you who haven't yet met her. She was the one who had the original vision warning us of what Satan's Spawn was plotting. She and I got together this morning to compare her visions with the dream I had last night." Standing at his side was a beautiful, raven-haired woman, dressed in a bright-colored flowing skirt and blouse, no taller than the middle of Seer's chest. This was the other "sprite" that Ghost had mentioned.

"In my dream," related Seer, "I saw Rat telling his men that half of the club would ride into the east side of town. They would create chaos by breaking windows, robbing businesses, and starting fires, while the other group would come in from the west and attack our compound. They would kill all who tried to stop them, whether a townie or Warrior.

"Rat and his group have no qualms killing innocents. They only care to take what is ours in any way they can. Oracle has confirmed this is also what she has seen in her visions. However, she feels that, if we are prepared, the outcomes will be good. With this advance information, we can solidify our strategy.

"Spokes, have you heard from your cook friend?"

"Yes. He and two of his helpers will be here this afternoon. I also told them what they would be facing, and they said to bring it on.

"When Tater Tot and his helpers arrive, I'll let you know, Seer," Spokes said. "I'll show them around the compound, the kitchen, pantries, storerooms, medical rooms, and where they will be sleeping. Once they check out the pantries, if they need anything not already there, I'll make a run to the stores. That way, they can jump in with both feet, hit the ground running, and get started on making the meals."

"That's good, because the visions say Rat will make his move in the next few days," Seer informed everyone.

The room erupted when this was reported and it took Seer's powerful voice and banging his gavel to quiet the room.

CHAPTER 8

"Last night, I asked if anyone had ideas on how we should move from our defensive mode to an offensive one. The floor is now open for discussion."

Torch spoke up first. "We need to make the town aware of what is going down and make them safe. At least the ones closest to our businesses and compounds. I don't think the Spawn will bother with anyone else, as they're too fixated on wiping us out. That also means we need to let the local law know—if you haven't done that already, Seer."

"Yes, both the Sheriff's Department and local cops have been informed. The impression I got from both departments was that they hope we will wipe each other out—then they'll only have to deal with what is left," Seer growled.

Next to speak up was Roar. "They will be coming in riding their bikes. The Elementals—Windy, Rain, Flame, and Terra—will brew up a storm they will never forget. They can blow them right off their bikes, drown them with rain, or even have lightning fry their asses. Flame can burn their bikes until nothing but piles of ash show where they fell. Then Terra can open a crevasse, dump them in and cover over any sign they were even there. Those who are lucky enough to get past them, you can deal with."

"After you take the starch out of them, it shouldn't be too hard to take the rest of them out," Viper snickered.

"Don't get too cocky, Viper. They're still dangerous," reminded Seer.

"If they do make it through the Elementals, Ghost and I can pick them up on the security cameras we've set up. Even if they try to take cover in the buildings, we can still find them. We can also hack into the traffic cams if needed," Wire interjected.

"Since we have two rapid-response teams, we can have one at the east end of town and one based at the compounds. That way, they can pounce on any fires or other damage the Spawn might try to inflict and care for anyone who is injured," Roar proposed.

"I also suggest everyone be equipped with earbuds. That way, we would be able to communicate with each other and with the teams," Wire mentioned.

"Sounds like a plan," Seer informed everyone. "Does anyone have anything to add?"

Flame told everyone that Torch and she had placed Molotov cocktails and fire extinguishers around each of the compounds and where they were located, so that members could grab them and use them as needed.

"Thanks for that information, Flame," said Seer.

"Okay, everyone finish whatever you need to finish, and try to get as much rest as you can. Things will start popping soon enough.

"Church dismissed."

CHAPTER 9

"Waiting is a pain," Flame complained.

"I can think of things to do to take your mind off those thoughts," offered Torch. "How about we pack a lunch, load up Woof, take the bikes out and spend some time together? I have a very special place I want to share with you. It's a quiet place, where we can just relax. This may be our last chance before all hell breaks loose. I want us to be able to clear our heads so to be ready to do battle."

"That's a wonderful idea," Flame sighed. "Let's do it."

After they rode for an hour, Torch had us turn onto a dirt road that wound around the mountain and ended at a hidden lake, protected by high canyon walls and an open meadow filled with wildflowers.

"Oh, this is so beautiful and peaceful. The world seems so far away," Flame said in awe as she gazed across the expanse. "How did you ever find this?"

"Riding the back roads and just exploring. I've kept this secret; I come here to unwind when things are weighing me down," explained

Torch. "I've never shared this with anyone before. You are the first, and I knew you would love it, too."

"I'm so glad you shared this with me, especially now that things are so heavy," she said happily.

"Let's unload the picnic things and let Woof explore. Maybe we can enjoy the lake before lunch—let our hair down. I can make love to my woman in a field of wildflowers," Torch grinned.

After they spent the day lying next to the crystal-clear water of the mountain lake, making love in the open air and sunshine, surrounded by wildflowers, and eating their fill of the picnic lunch, they collected Woof, loaded the bikes, and started the long ride back.

Once they reached the compound, Flame and Torch everyone outside the Warriors' clubhouse with a drink in their hand, milling around the picnic tables, talking and laughing. Tater Tot, the new cook, and his two friends and assistants, Adam and Zak, had arrived earlier that day and were manning the outdoor grills, where tantalizing smells were scenting the air.

Looking at each other and grinning, Torch chuckled, "Guess we will be eating here tonight," as both our stomachs started grumbling and mouths began watering.

They each took a plate and loaded it with ribs and sides of potato salad and beans, and picked up a drink from the ice-filled tubs, before they headed over to where Seer was sitting and eating with Roar and Oracle.

"This is just the calm before the storm," Seer commented, grimly. "We sent out some Prospects to watch for any activity on I-10, both east and west, heading our way from Lordsburg. They will call it in when they do. That should allow a couple of hours, at least, for us to firm up everything and get people set and ready. I fully expect them to arrive sometime in the late morning or afternoon tomorrow. So, eat up, get some rest, and we will meet up again for breakfast." Seer, Roar, and Oracle picked up their plates and left.

After they heard this, Torch and Flame finished their meal and walked slowly toward the hotel, while Woof sniffed around before he did his business. They discussed what Seer said before they entered their suite. Their clothes were thrown off as they made love in the shower and again in the king-sized bed, enjoying and memorizing the other's body before collapsing and falling to sleep.

CHAPTER 10

Once an outstanding breakfast of egg, bacon, mushroom casserole, sourdough toast, and freshly brewed coffee and tea was consumed, Seer's cell phone rang. The room went silent. "Yeah, okay. How many? When did they pass you? Okay, head on back, but don't let them see you. If anything changes, let us know."

"Church, *now*!" yelled Seer. Plates, knives, forks, and cups were abandoned with a clatter. Once everyone was seated, Seer told them, "Here's the scoop. The Prospect says Rat and about 30 of Satan's Spawn passed him, heading our way. He will follow and make sure they don't change their route. If they do, he'll let us know. He figures that, at the speed they're riding at, they should arrive around 11 a.m. if they don't stop to fill up or change the route.

"Is everyone clear on their assignments? If so, take your positions on the east side. Compounds are now on lockdown. Expect the action to begin in about two hours—or less!

"Any questions? No? Church dismissed."

Flame kissed Torch deeply and gave her brother a hug, then headed to the east with the other Elementals and Rapid Response Team #1. Seer, Torch, the other club brothers, and the Rapid Response Team #2 stayed to defend the compounds, telling each other to stay safe. Tater Tot, Adam, and Zak picked up the forgotten plates, utensils, and glasses to prepare the space for the next time it was needed.

The minutes slowly ticked by until the women and RRT #1 heard the loud roar of motorcycles. The sound grew louder and louder as the enemy drew near.

From their earbuds, they heard Roar yell, "Now is the time, Elementals, to give them hell! Give them a storm they will never forget!"

With that, Windy unleashed tornado-strength winds strong enough it blew them off their bikes. Torrential bands of rain started, and lightning made it difficult to see the road. Terra added to the mayhem by making both crevasses and berms that the enemy would either have to jump or fall into. Flame came behind to incinerate the fallen bikes thus no escape was left except on foot.

Roar followed up by sending in Rapid Response Team #1 to restrain the fallen, pull out those from in the crevasses that Terra made in the road, and to track down the rabbits.

When the action died down, Roar informed Seer, "We have 15 bodies here. They are either restrained or dead, or soon will be. No casualties on our side but broken bones, broken necks, and various lacerations and contusions on their part. I'll leave RRT #1 here to watch over this scum. and we can move your way. How's it going at the compounds?"

"They're coming in quietly, having parked their bikes down the road, out of sight," said Seer.

"We have eyes on them due to Wire sending a drone up. Torch, Mountain, and Cyclone are biding their time until Rat shows up. Then, they will hit them with a fire and a windstorm, if needed, while Mountain chucks rocks at them," Seer laughed.

"If things are secure, roads clear, and any damage repaired on the east side, then you and the women can join in the fun here. Maybe take care of their bikes so they can't use them to retreat," he suggested.

"Roger that," Roar responded. "Okay, everyone. Flame, you and Terra need to get to their bikes and make it so they can't escape. I'll leave that up to you to decide," she smiled evilly. "Rain, you and Windy come with me to the hotel. Rat will be concentrating on the Warriors' compound, but I want to make sure they don't try anything on ours or try to seek safety there. If they do, they'll get the surprise of a lifetime," Roar cackled. "Between you two and Woof, they don't stand a chance.

"We can watch what is happening outside the compounds on the monitors Ghost and Wire have set up. Let's join her and see if she has the feed from the drone we can watch."

Leaving members guarding the doors, Roar, Rain, and Windy joined Ghost to follow the action as it unfolded at the next compound.

CHAPTER 11

As he tapped twice on his earbud, Torch signaled Rat's approach to Seer.

Rat and five of his men carried heavy gas canisters, while the remainder were spread out to the sides. Each man had a weapon in his hands. Rat nodded, and he began to pour gas along the fence and guard shack of the Warrior compound.

Torch shouted from his well-hidden position, "Bad idea, Rat. Very, very, very bad idea. You have chosen the wrong club and wrong territory to try to take over."

Rat turned at the sound of Torch's voice, and his men started laying a barrage of bullets in the direction from where the voice was heard, but Torch had already moved to a new position.

Rat chose that moment to strike a match. Instead of Rat setting fire to the compound, Torch sent a flame to the trail of gas and up to the canister that Rat still held. As the flame reached the canister of fuel, it exploded, covering Rat with fuel and flames.

Screaming as his clothing and hair caught fire, Rat raced down the road and collapsed. Dead and smoldering.

The remainder of the gang stared in shock at their fallen President. With no fight left in them, the remaining Spawn placed the canisters of fuel and guns down. The VP, Snarl, raised his hands and shouted, "I did not agree with Rat about taking over your territory. I have nothing against your club. Just let us go, and we will leave and not bother your club again."

"Oh, no—it's not going to be that easy," stated Seer, coming through the gates. "You and your brothers made threats against our club, our businesses, and our town. You had every intention of destroying all we worked hard to build. You planned to kill all of us and then walk in and take over.

"You were going to launch a two-pronged attack from the east to burn and kill everyone there, while Rat led your group on our compound. Just because you didn't succeed doesn't mean you get off scot-free."

"The sheriff and Denton police have picked up your brothers—or what's left of them—from the east side. They are now headed here to arrest you and what is left of your club brothers, and to scoop up the remains of your dearly departed President."

CHAPTER 12

While the club Presidents, Seer and Roar, sat outside the Warriors clubhouse with a beer in their hands, they watched both of the clubs' members relax and celebrate. Seer turned to Roar and mused, "This could have turned out so differently without you and the other women. Without Oracle and the Elemental Spirits, we wouldn't have known in time what Rat had planned. Oracle was right—we would have been wiped out, because we didn't have the manpower to cover both ends of town. My dream came too late to fully understand what danger we were in, and I still don't know why I wasn't able to pick up the threat earlier.

"We would not have had the defenses built up, nor would we have been strong enough, even with our special gifts, skills, and training, to withstand the attacks. We would have been spread too thin to be effective.

"I'm sure there would have been more injured or killed without your help. For that and for getting to know my sister and her club better, I sincerely thank you."

"You're welcome," returned Roar. "In helping you, we have met a wonderful and gifted group of men that we can be ourselves around. We don't have to worry that those gifts need to be hidden any longer but can be openly used and appreciated."

"We have a beautiful new clubhouse that we can defend if needed. A friendly town where we can build our businesses and thrive. So, I need to thank you again. That being said, let's party!"

EPILOGUE

As time passed, the Satan's Spawn were disbanded and whatever members who managed to survive that night were tried and sentenced to a maximum of 40 years for attempted murder, assault, and attempted arson. Rat's death was ruled a self-inflicted accident. Seemed when he was pouring the fuel on the guard shack, he spilled some gas on himself, and, by lighting the match, it caused his clothing to catch on fire, which led to his death. Good riddance.

Flame set up her fabrication shop and worked her dream job of designing specialty bikes and tanks, and displaying welded art around town and in her gallery. Torch and Flame plan on a fall wedding and to start a family within the next year. The first new home would be built within the compound, but more would follow. The siblings decided to take the fence down between the two compounds and blend them to allow both clubs freer access. Each club would still have their own clubhouses, rooms and suites. Flame and her brother got closer than they had ever been before and spent long periods of time together, just talking and exchanging family stories.

Both clubs' businesses expanded and grew, as did the clubs. New members joined and started their own shops. It seemed the clubs drew people who were "special."

Dex has joined forces to partner in the construction company with Mountain. Oracle has opened a specialty bakery cafe serving artisan breads, soups, and sandwiches. There were even plans in the works for Tater Tot to open a restaurant and allow the Prospects to handle the day-to-day meals at the compounds.

Wire and Ghost and a few of the military brothers and sisters formed a security service. It took off and rapidly became *the* place to go for simple IT problems, protections against corporate espionage, or even personal-protection needs.

The clubs have remained close. More and more of the members become couples. A regular subdivision was laid out for future homes, thus assuring Mountain and Dex's company would be kept busy building. With the fence taken down that divided the two clubs, there were more lots available.

Seer and Oracle have not had any disturbing or threatening dreams or visions. Fingers-crossed, it would remain that way. However, the future was still uncharted, and many things could affect it. So, everyone stayed vigilant, as no one knew when their skills and gifts would be needed again.